ALI B.
and the
Forty Thieves

Level 3

Retold by Fiona Kalinowski

Series Editors: Annie Hughes and Melanie Williams

Touag Rasha

Pearson Education Limited
Edinburgh Gate, Harlow
Essex CM20 2JE, England
and Associated Companies throughout the world.

ISBN-13: 978-0-582-43097-6
ISBN-10: 0-582-43097-6

First published by Librairie du Liban Publishers,1996
This adaptation first published 2000 under licence by
Penguin Books
2000 © Penguin Books Ltd
Illustrations © 1996 Librairie du Liban

7 9 10 8

Illustrations by Angus McBride
Design by Traffika Publishing/Wendi Watson

Printed in China
SWTC/07

Published by Pearson Education Limited in association with Penguin Books Ltd,
both companies being subsidiaries of Pearson Plc

For a complete list of titles available in the Penguin Young Readers
series please write to your local Pearson Education office or contact:
Penguin Readers Marketing Department, Pearson Education,
Edinburgh Gate, Harlow, Essex, CM20 2JE.

Once upon a time, a long time ago, in the country of sun, sand and pyramids, there lived a poor man. Ali Baba, for that was his name, was poor but he was happy.

He had a kind wife and a beautiful and clever daughter named Leia. They lived in a small yellow stone house in a small town near some hills.

There were many trees in these hills and every day Ali Baba went there to cut wood. He rode to the hills on his donkey, cut the wood, put it on the donkey's back and rode back to the town to sell it at the market.

One day when he was cutting wood, Ali Baba heard the sound of some horses. They were coming up the hill.

'Horses!' he thought. 'Horses and men. I have to hide.'

Quickly he climbed a tree and hid in the green leaves. Soon he saw the men and the horses. They stopped near his tree. All the men were carrying bags. They looked fierce and dangerous and Ali Baba knew that they were thieves.

The leader of the thieves went up and stood in front of a big round stone. He put up his hands and cried, 'Open Sesame'.

The stone opened slowly and Ali Baba could see a cave. It was big and very dark.

Quickly the thieves put their bags in the cave. Then the leader put up his hands again and said loudly, 'Close Sesame'. The stone moved slowly back. The men got on their horses and rode away.

Ali Baba waited in the tree until he could no longer hear the sound of the horses. He was still afraid but he climbed down and walked over to the stone.

He put up his hands and whispered, 'Open Sesame'.

The stone moved and Ali Baba walked into the cave. He could not believe his eyes!

The cave was full of gold and silver.
Everywhere he looked he saw gold, gold
boxes, gold animals, and bags
of gold and silver.

Quickly Ali Baba took a bag of gold coins and ran out of the cave.

'Close Sesame!' he cried and the stone moved back slowly.

He ran to his donkey, which was still hiding in the trees, put the gold on its back, and rode home as fast as he could.

'Look what I have found,' he cried to his wife. When she looked in the bag, her eyes grew round with surprise.

Gold coins!' she said. 'Hundreds of gold coins! Ali Baba, where did you get them?'

Ali Baba told her about the thieves and the stone and the cave full of gold and silver. 'Oh, we are going to get rich,' she said. 'Leia,' she cried to her daughter. 'Leia, come here. Come and see what your father has found.'

When Leia saw the gold coins, she said happily, 'I will go and get the weighing scales from Aunt Kasima. We need to know how much they weigh. Then we will know how rich we are.'

She went quickly and came back with the scales.

13

Ali Baba's wife
weighed the coins.
'Oh, we are rich, very,
very rich! We will buy a
new house, and I will buy
new clothes for all of us.
Leia, take the scales
back to your aunt and
give her this gold coin.'

That evening, Aunt
Kasima showed the
coin to her husband, Ali
Baba's brother, Kasim.
'Look,' she said. 'Look
what we got from your
brother.'
Kasim looked at
the gold coin and
whispered, 'Oh no,
is my brother a thief?'

That night he did not sleep well. Next
morning he went to talk to his brother.
'Ali Baba, where did you get this gold coin?'
he asked. 'Are you a thief?'
Ali Baba laughed. 'No brother, I'm not a
thief, but I've found a cave where thieves
hide their gold.'

He told Kasim about the cave and the
thieves and the gold. He told him about
the stone.
'I will take you there tomorrow,' he said.

Kasim went home to work but all morning he thought about the cave and the gold.
'I don't want to wait until tomorrow, I can't wait until tomorrow!' he thought.

So in the afternoon he rode quickly to the cave by himself.

He stood in front of the stone and said, 'Open Sesame'.
The stone moved and Kasim walked into the cave.

Everywhere he looked he saw gold.
'Gold! So much gold!' he cried.
'Oh, I'm rich, very rich.'

Suddenly he heard the sound of horses outside the cave. He tried to hide, but he was too late. The thieves, forty of them, came into the cave.

When they saw Kasim, they took out their long knives.

'Who are you?' cried the leader. 'What are you doing in our cave? Catch him, men. He is trying to steal our gold.'

19

'Please, please don't kill me!'
Kasim cried. He was very, very scared.

'I didn't want to take your gold. I was just looking. My brother, Ali Baba, told me it was here. He found the cave and took some gold. Please, please don't kill me.'

The leader of the thieves said, 'Tell us where your brother lives, and you can go home.'

But when Kasim told him, he laughed a terrible laugh.

'Tie him up men. We will find this Ali Baba and our gold. Then we will kill him and his brother.'

The leader told the thieves to get forty big oil jars.

'Men, I'm going to put oil in one jar and you are going to hide in the other jars. I will take the jars to Ali Baba's house. Then, in the middle of the night, when everyone is sleeping, I will open the jars. You will climb out and kill Ali Baba and his family and we will get our gold back.'

Then the leader put oil in one jar and the thirty-nine thieves climbed into the other thirty-nine jars.

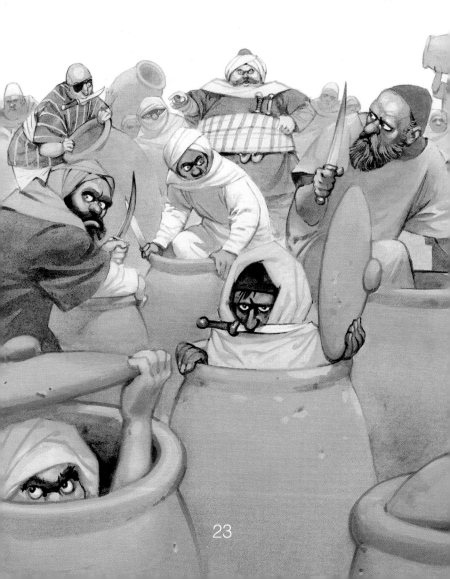

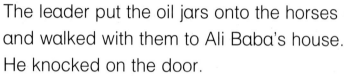

The leader put the oil jars onto the horses
and walked with them to Ali Baba's house.
He knocked on the door.
'Good evening, kind friend. Can you help
me, please? I have come from far away to
sell my oil at the market. It's now
evening and the
market is closed.

24

Please, can my horses and my oil jars stay in your garden until the morning?'
'Oh, yes, they can stay here,' said Ali Baba, for he was a kind man and he was always happy to help people.

'And you can sleep in my house,' he said to the leader.

Little did Ali Baba know what the thieves were planning.

After dinner, the leader of the thieves went into the garden to speak to his men. 'Remember,' he whispered into the jars.

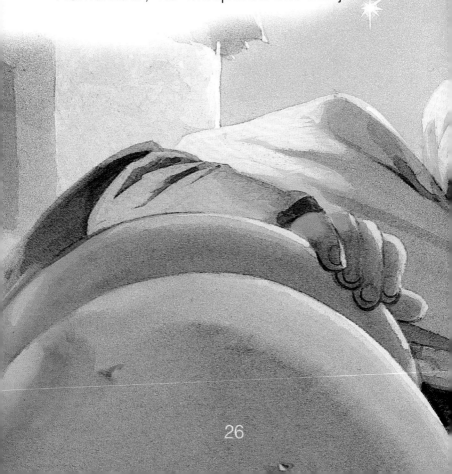

'In the night, when I open your jar, climb out, go into the house, kill Ali Baba and his family, and find our gold.'

Later that evening, Leia went to get some
oil. It was very quiet in the garden.

Suddenly she heard whispers from the jars.
'It's cold in here.'
'I need to move.'

Leia listened and understood.
'The thieves from the cave are in these jars.
I'll teach them a lesson,' she thought.

In the house she made some oil very hot.
Then she put a little in every jar.

'Oh, ouch,' cried the thieves. One by one they jumped out of the jars and ran away as fast as they could. Their leader ran away too.

They were so scared, they ran for a long time before they stopped. They did not come back to Ali Baba's house and they never went back to their cave again.

A few days later, when Ali Baba was sure that the thieves were not coming back, he went to the cave and found his brother Kasim, cold, afraid, but living.

They cried together and then they laughed together. Then they took some more gold and went home.

The two families and all their friends were now very rich and lived happily ever after.

Activities

Before you read

I. Look at the picture on the front of the book.
   a. Who do you think this is?
   b. What is he looking at?
   c. Where he is looking?

2. Now look at the pictures in the book.
   a. What country do you think Ali Baba lived in?
   b. Why do you think this?
   c. What language do you think he spoke?
   d. Did Ali Baba live in the country or in a town?
   e. Why do you think this?
   f. What are thieves?
   g. What did forty thieves steal?

After you read

I. Find the words in this sentence about the story.
   <u>Underline</u> them.
   Then write the sentence again.
   Theleaderclosedthejarsandputthemonthehorses.

2. Can you match the opposites?

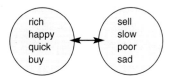

3. Now draw pictures to show one pair of opposites. Show them to your friends. Can they guess what the opposites are?

4. Here are 10 words from the story. Can you find them in the square below?

wood, coins, thieves, leader, gold, jars, stone, cave, oil, pyramid

j	t	s	k	v	b	c	o	i	l
a	w	o	o	d	n	o	h	x	c
r	y	d	l	q	m	i	j	v	t
s	u	f	s	t	o	n	e	b	h
f	i	g	z	w	g	s	k	c	i
l	e	a	d	e	r	a	l	a	e
q	o	h	x	e	f	s	z	v	v
w	p	y	r	a	m	i	d	e	e
e	p	j	c	r	t	y	u	n	s
r	a	g	o	l	d	d	i	o	p

5. Here is a newspaper story about Leia and the thieves but it is not finished. Putting some of the words below in the empty spaces, can you finish it?

heard, happy, hot, climbing, burned, his, jars, clever, garden, scared, her, hiding, in, ran

Yesterday, Leia Baba, a — girl from this town, — away some thieves from — father's house. They were — in some oil jars — the garden, but Leia — them. She put some oil in every jar and — them. They jumped out of the — and ran away. Well done Leia!